THE PEASANT AND THE FLY

Osmond Molarsky

THE PEASANT AND THE FLY

ILLUSTRATED BY KATHERINE COVILLE

HARCOURT
BRACE
JOVANOVICH

NEW YORK
AND
LONDON

For my brother

Printed in the United States of America

LIBRARY OF CONGRESS CATALOGING IN PUBLICATION DATA
Molarsky, Osmond.
The peasant and the fly.
SUMMARY: An inventive peasant shows Tsar Dimitri the Foolish
how to rid himself of an annoying fly.
[1. Kings, queens, rulers, etc.—Fiction 2. Flies—Fiction]
I. Coville, Katherine.   II. Title.
PZ7.M7317Pe   [Fic]   80–11609
ISBN 0–15–260152–X   ISBN 0–15–260153–8 pbk.

Set in Videocomp Garamond
First Edition
B   C   D   E

Many years ago, during the reign of Tsar Dimitri the Foolish, there lived in the village of Timsk, deep in the central part of Mother Russia, a peasant named Pirigov. He was not a poor peasant because he was very clever and found many ways to make life for himself and his family easy and comfortable. Pirigov grew more cabbages and bigger turnips than any other peasant in the whole village, so on market day his wife came home with a jingle of coins in her apron pocket or perhaps a fine cheese or a fat goose she had bought with the profits.

Pirigov was clever in other ways, as well. He discovered, for example, that it was easier to raise a heavy pail of water from a deep well with a crank than to haul it up, hand over hand.

He discovered that he could make the scarecrow in his garden do a constant jig and keep crows away from the newly planted carrots by attaching a long string to the baby's cradle, which was almost always being rocked by an older child.

And it was a wonder to the other peasants how fast Pirigov and his family could gather cranberries in the cranberry bog until they saw the many-toothed, comblike scoops the Pirigovs used to separate the firm red berries from their stems. Pirigov had thought the scoops up himself and had made them from birchwood. He did not try to keep his discoveries secret but shared them with others in his village and in other villages on the great estate, thus making easier the lives and lightening the work of many besides himself.

Now while Pirigov was making his clever inventions in the village of Timsk, far away in the great city of Moscva, Tsar Dimitri the Foolish ruled over the land with the help of many counselors, every one of them just as foolish as he. Whether or not they were all really that foolish is hard to say. It is possible that one or two just acted that way so as not to show up the Tsar and get their heads chopped off for being too smart.

Counsel was given in the great council hall, with the Tsar on his throne and the counselors seated at a long table at its foot. The Tsar would tell his problems to the counselors, and they would answer in turn, according to their rank.

On this particular day, the Tsar needed advice on several matters. For one thing, the royal bedstead had developed a squeak that made itself heard every time the Tsar or his wife, the Tsarina, turned over. It did not trouble the Tsarina, who was a very sound sleeper. No noise could wake her. But every time the bed squeaked, it awakened the Tsar, and he found it very difficult to go back to sleep.

He was often very tired and ill-natured for the whole day unless he could catch a nap on the small couch in the anteroom of the great council hall. The entire council went up to inspect the bed and, after some consultation, promised to solve the problem by the end of the month.

Next was the matter of the soaring price of shoes. Shoes cost so much that common people simply could not afford them, and many of the Tsar's loyal subjects had to walk around with holes in their soles. The counselors put their heads together around the table and discussed the problem for ten minutes or so. At the end of this time, the head counselor said, "Your Exalted Highness, this is our advice. Let the people stop wearing shoes. In the summer, they don't need them because it is warm. In winter, their feet will very quickly become numb from the cold, so they won't know whether they are wearing shoes or not. The counselors, of course, each had at least one pair of good shoes and another for second best. The Tsar thought about their answer for a few minutes, then sent for his chief herald, and soon the order was spread across the land. "Shoes shall not be worn by people who cannot afford them." It was one of the laws that helped earn the Tsar his name, the Foolish.

Now, while the counselors were thinking about these problems and advising the Tsar, a fly had somehow gotten into the great council hall. This was strictly against palace rules and regulations, which were posted in large letters and in several languages where everyone could see them. Nevertheless, a fly was inside and was fiercely buzzing and zooming around the Tsar, doing figure eights, loop-the-loops, and power dives.

At first the Tsar paid no attention to the bothersome fly. "A Tsar of all the Russias does not notice a humble fly," he told himself.

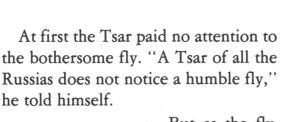

But as the fly kept getting closer, zooming about his nose, buzzing one ear and then the other, swooping at his left eye three times in a row, then alighting on his beard, the Tsar finally could control himself no longer, and he lifted a royal hand to brush it off.

The fly, which of course could see in all directions, was one jump ahead of the Tsar and was buzzing circles around that monarch's crown almost before he was able to raise his hand.

Finally the Tsar lost his temper and let out a roar that echoed around the great council chamber and throughout the palace.

"Who let this fly in!" he bellowed.

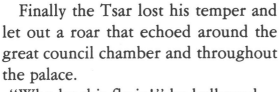

Of course, no one answered. The penalty for admitting flies was severe. "Never mind," he said, then shouted, "Captain of the guard!"

Within seconds, the captain of the guard was standing before the Tsar at strict attention. "I condemn this fly to death!" the Tsar decreed. "Arrest it at once and have it executed without delay."

The captain of the guard saluted smartly and said, "I'll call my men." Then, pivoting on his heel, he commanded, "Men! On the double!"

With a great pounding of boots, jangling of spurs, and rattling of swords, the entire platoon of guardsmen clattered into the great council chamber and came to attention before the Tsar.

"Corporal Karpovich!" the captain of the guard commanded. "Arrest that fly sitting on the imperial nose."

Corporal Karpovich stepped forward and saluted his captain. Then, to his squad, he gave an order. "Squad—two steps forward." As the four men advanced and stood at attention, he commanded, "Arrest that fly!"

The guardsmen, who were not very brave underneath their red, gold, and black velvet uniforms, polished boots, and snow white gloves, approached the Tsar as mice would approach a cat. It frightened them just to be near the mighty monarch. As for arresting the fly that had perched on the end of his nose, that was a very dangerous mission indeed. An army of Tartars would have been more to their liking.

For his part, the Tsar dared not make an untsarlike move in the presence of the guard, so he just sat there, still as a toy stuffed bear. Only his eyes moved, turning slowly toward his nose, where the fly had lit.

"Seize him!" the corporal commanded and like well-drilled guardsmen, all four of them made a grab for the condemned insect.

The Tsar, who was only human, ducked, and a lucky thing it was, or the royal nose would have taken a painful drubbing. The guardsmen now withdrew in disgrace to their places in the platoon. They had failed to arrest the fly as Tsar Dimitri the Foolish had ordered and their captain had commanded.

The fly had escaped unharmed and was flying about the great council hall in wide figure eights, buzzing and humming. Being condemned meant nothing to the fly. To execute it, they must first catch it. And it had them there. So sure of itself was that fly that straightway again it began to buzz the Tsar more furiously than before. It zoomed and looped and dived about his eyebrows. It zigged past his ear and zagged over his nose and around his beard, slowly driving the Tsar Dimitri the Foolish mad. Something had to be done.

"Attention, guardsmen!" It was the captain again. "A call for volunteers. Volunteers . . . one step forward . . . march!" The entire guard stepped forward, except of course the four men who had just failed to capture the culprit and were now looking down at their boots in shame. The captain looked proud—not a coward in the lot. "Draw . . . sabers!" he commanded, then, "Attack!"

Such a fierce slashing and cutting of sabers, scooping of the
air with plumed hats, and grasping of air around the Tsar's
head had never been seen, as the fly continued to loop and
zoom around the monarch. Several retreats were ordered so

the guard could regroup, and as many attacks were launched
and launched again. Several guardsmen were wounded and
blood flowed, but the wounds were bandaged, and the men
returned to the attack as good as new.

Then suddenly in the heat of battle, one of the guardsmen noticed that they were fighting nothing. The fly was gone. For a moment, the captain was dismayed. He had let the culprit escape. Then, gathering his wits and standing very straight, he ordered the guard to fall into line and stand at attention. To the Tsar, he announced, "My men have defeated the enemy. The fly has fled. We are in command of the field. Your excellency is safe. My men are sworn to protect your excellency's person, and we have done our duty—men, you have done your duty."

Recovered from his own confusion, the Tsar replied, "Yes. Indeed. Thank you very much. I shall order medals for valor—one to a man. Dismissed."

"Right . . . face!" the captain of the guard commanded. "Forward . . . march!" And with that the guard trooped out, sabers clanking and boots clicking on the polished marble floor of the council hall. One man alone had removed his plumed hat and was looking inside to see if just maybe he had captured the fly.

That of course was not the end of the matter. Next day, the Tsar and his counselors were considering the problem of the Ulm River, which had overflowed its banks in the spring thaw and had wreaked much damage. The third counselor had just suggested that they drill a hole in the bottom of the river to let the water out.

The Tsar was scratching his head, thinking about it, when BUZZZZZZZZ! In zoomed the fly and began all over again pestering and tormenting his excellency. Where the fly had gone during the skirmish or where he had spent the night, no one knew. Only one thing was certain. The fly had returned, undaunted by the slashing sabers of the Tsar's guard.

Now, the Tsar may have been foolish, but he was not so foolish as to call the guard again. In fact, he canceled the order for the medals then and there. Instead, he asked for suggestions from his counselors. "How do I get rid of this fly, once and for all?" he wanted to know.

There was no end of suggestions, and some were tried. Enclose the Tsar in a box covered with a fine veil (they had no window screens in those days).

Appoint the fly to the council.

Give it a medal and a pension for life.

"No bribery, please," said the Tsar, who, though foolish, was honest.

One of the counselors seated near the foot of the table doodled out on his scratch pad the design for a kind of paddle that might be used to swat a fly dead. But he gave up that idea when he noticed that practically the only place where the fly ever lit was on some tender part of the Tsar's person. Who would be brave enough to swat the Tsar on a tender place, even to kill the fly?

The fly returned each day to the council chamber and kept the place in a constant uproar so that very little counsel was ever given, even on important questions, and the business of running the nation was coming to a standstill. Even the war with a neighboring country had to be put off until a later date.

Now, as usually happens in cases of this kind, the Tsar at last decided to send his heralds throughout the land to seek some man or woman or even a child with special wisdom on how to rid the Tsar of the infernal fly. Heralds spread the word in the large cities, where they found no one at all with the wisdom to solve the problem. They tried the towns, where the city fathers met to study the problem but failed to find the answer.

Then, in a last, hopeless effort, the heralds of the Tsar fanned out over the land to the tiny villages that dotted the great estates and plantations of the nobles. One day, coming to the village of Timsk, a herald sounded his trumpet and proclaimed his message for one and all to hear. "Who in the land knows how to capture the insolent fly that is plaguing the Tsar of all the Russias?"

"The man for you to see is Pirigov," the villagers said.

"Why?" asked the herald, doubting a peasant could solve the Tsar's problem.

"Because he is clever and wise. His inventions have helped everyone in this village and for miles around. He can help the Tsar."

"Where is this Pirigov, then? I wish to see him."

"He is out in his field, harvesting wheat with a beautiful knife he made in the shape of a new moon. He calls it a sickle. Ah, but here he comes now."

With his wonderful new sickle, Pirigov had finished his work in the field early. Now he approached the crowd of villagers, wondering at the figure seated on horseback in their midst, so richly attired, with the Tsar's seal emblazoned on his wallet.

"Here he is! The man who can rid the Tsar of the insolent fly!" the villagers cried proudly. Then, all talking at once, they explained the Tsar's problem to Pirigov.

"Can you capture the fly?" the herald demanded.

"I can promise nothing," said Pirigov. "But come to my cottage and make up your own mind."

At the cottage, Pirigov cranked up a bucket of clear, cold water from the well. "Please help yourself to a drink," the peasant said.

"Amazing," said the thirsty herald, between gulps. "What do you call that thing?"

"A windlass," said the peasant Pirigov.

"I shall have to tell the Tsar's engineers about it."

Nearby in the garden, a scarecrow was jigging about, frightening crows.

"What makes it jig?" the herald wanted to know. Pirigov pointed to the cradle with a baby in it.

"There is almost always a baby in the cradle," said Pirigov's wife.

"Amazing," said the herald. "What other wonderful things have you invented?"

Pirigov's wife showed him the turnip grater her husband had fashioned of very hard wood, the middle daughter, Katya, proudly displayed the cranberry picker, and Alyosha, Grigory, and Grushenka brought out other simple, useful things their father had made. "Astonishing!" exclaimed the herald. "I shall take a chance. Be ready to leave for Moscva in ten minutes," he commanded. "A royal carriage is waiting in the village square."

After seven days and seven nights of riding, Pirigov arrived at the nation's capital, a little tired but ready to help the Tsar in his time of trouble.

The Tsar and his council were meeting in the great council hall. The fly was buzzing the Tsar, who looked old and haggard. The herald, still dusty from the long journey, stepped through the great doors, raised his trumpet, blew a ringing blast, and cried out in his shrillest voice, "The peasant Pirigov!"

Pirigov strode boldly into the royal presence, bowed low to the Tsar, and said, "The peasant Pirigov at the service of Tsar and country!" This was not the way a simple peasant would have talked normally, but during the long journey, the herald had given Pirigov lessons in how to behave at court, and now he was doing just what the herald had taught him—adding a few touches of his own, as was his nature.

Slapping at the fly, which had just lit on his right eyebrow, the Tsar looked down on Pirigov, observed his rough clothing and unpolished boots, and said, "What is this? Who is this . . . this person?"

"The man who will capture the fly, Your Highness," the herald announced and blew his trumpet again to prove to the Tsar that what he said was true.

At that, a loud whisper arose from the council table. Would a simple peasant show them up for fools? A wise man from beyond the Ural Mountains, perhaps, but a simple peasant? Never!

During the uproar, Pirigov, who was not so simple and who found that he enjoyed acting like a courtier, turned to the council table and bowed low. What could the counselors do? Nothing. And that was what they did.

"Capture the fly, then, peasant!" Tsar Dimitri the Foolish commanded.

"My pleasure, Your Highness," said Pirigov, who had been studying the situation in the great council hall. "But first I must have three things."

"Name them, and they shall be yours," said the Tsar, swatting himself on the beard.

"First," said Pirigov, "I must have a pot of honey."

"A pot of money?" asked the Tsar, who did not hear well.

"A pot of *honey*. Money would be of no help whatsoever."

"Fetch a pot of honey from the royal pantry," the Tsar ordered, and several footmen hurried off to the pantry. "What else?" asked the Tsar.

"A strip of cloth, about so long and so wide," Pirigov said.

"Go to the sewing room, where the Tsarina is sewing me a nightshirt, and ask her for a strip of the finest linen," the Tsar commanded, and a flock of flunkeys clattered off toward the royal sewing room.

Meanwhile, Pirigov was studying the great chandelier that hung directly above the crowned head of the Tsar.

"The last thing," he said, "is a long piece of string." The monarch pushed back his crown and scratched his head.

Then he remembered. "Fetch the string bag," he directed. "It's hanging just inside the wardrobe door. Hurry!" And off scampered three of the pages to find it.

As Pirigov waited, he took from his pocket a beautiful horse chestnut, smooth, dark brown, and polished. It was his good luck piece, and he kept it with him always. Now, as the pages returned with the string, he bored a hole in the horse chestnut with his all-purpose knife, poked one end of the string through the chestnut, and tied a knot in it.

Then as counselors, flunkeys, pages, footmen, the herald, and the Tsar watched, he flung the chestnut up over the chandelier and let it down to within five feet of the monarch's crown. Then he tied the other end of the string to the back of the throne and, for the moment, let the chestnut swing in the air over the Tsar's head. So astonished was the Tsar that he forgot to brush away the fly, which was perched on his excellency's left ear, boldly grooming its wings with its two back legs.

By this time, the flunkeys and footmen had brought the jar of honey and the cloth.

"Thank you," Pirigov said. "This should do the trick. But of course I can't guarantee positively to catch the fly."

"You can't?" said the chief counselor, secretly hoping the peasant Pirigov would fail.

"It may just be that city flies are smarter than country flies. But I shall do my best." So saying, Pirigov tied the strip of cloth to the end of the string and dipped it deep into the honey. Next, he drew it out and let it drip and drain back into the pot until it would drip no more, or so he hoped.

Finally he hoisted high the sticky cloth until it dangled just above the Tsar. "All we can do now is wait," the peasant announced.

For at least five minutes, the fly buzzed the Tsar more furiously than ever, lighting on his nose and ear, cheek and beard, eyebrow and forehead, beard and nose. The Tsar was fuming. Then suddenly the fly zoomed off into the high vaulted places of the council hall and was lost to sight, as often happened. But it would surely return. No one doubted that. Then back it came, doing the loop-the-loops, figure eights, and every flying trick known to flies. But this

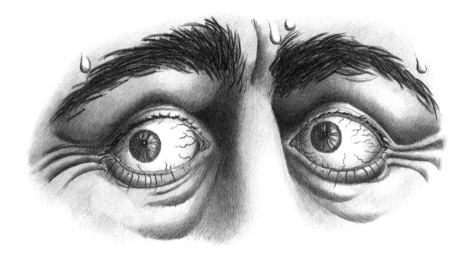

time there was a difference. The fly did not buzz the Tsar. It buzzed the strip of cloth hanging from the chandelier. Around and around the cloth the fly circled, looping and diving. But never once did it loop or dive near the Tsar or perform figure eights around his ears. Everyone watched to see what the fly would do. The Tsar watched. The counselors watched. The footmen, the flunkeys, the pages, and the herald watched. And Pirigov watched.

And they held their breaths.

The only thing that moved in the council chamber was the insolent fly, buzzing the strip of cloth hanging from the chandelier above the Tsar's crown.

All eyes moved, of course, to follow the fly. But only
eyes. Suddenly the fly swooped down once again at the
Tsar, zoomed up to the great arched ceilings, dived again,
and lit on the strip of cloth.

"Got him," Pirigov said quietly.

"Got him?" said the Tsar.

"Got him," said Pirigov. He reached up and cut down the cloth as the fly stayed where it was, all six feet stuck fast in the honey.

All in the great council hall let out their breaths. The fly had been caught. Now the guard trooped in, placed the fly under arrest, and bore it off to await its execution. The Tsar was a free man again, and the business of state could go forward. And although the Tsar's council had been shown up by a simple peasant and the guard had been defeated by a fly, all nevertheless were happy to have the problem solved at last.

The peasant Pirigov's reward? The Tsar offered him anything in the world, within reason, except the hand of his daughter. He had already bestowed several daughters upon brave or wise young men, and he felt that he should keep one daughter in reserve in case of some especially grave threat to the nation.

"That's all right, your excellency," the peasant said. "I already have a wife and seven children. It's been my pleasure to serve you. Just send me back to my village in the carriage that brought me here, and I shall be quite happy."

The Tsar asked the peasant to step outside for a few moments while he consulted with his counselors, then called him back and said, "It's not customary to let a loyal subject go unrewarded when he has done a wise or a brave deed. But if you wish it, so be it. But would you refuse a medal, just a small one, showing my face on one side and perhaps a pot of money—honey, that is—on the other?"

"That would be a very nice thing to have," Pirigov said. "I could wear it around my neck for good luck and show it around. Just send it along whenever it's convenient."

And so, seven days later Pirigov, the clever peasant, stepped out of the Tsar's carriage to find himself once again in front of his own house, in his own village, where he was greeted warmly by his wife, his seven children, and his proud neighbors. There things worked out for him as he deserved, and we may be sure that he and his family lived in the village of Timsk happily ever after, with Pirigov making only an occasional trip to Moscva to advise the Tsar on special matters.